OCCAM[

FANTASTIC BEASTS

DEMIGUISE

NIFFLER

MAGIZOOLOGIST

NEWT
SCAMANDER

NOTHING THAT OCCURS ... RE CAN BE UNNATURAL ... UNNATURAL ... NOTHING

FANTASTIC
BEASTS
AND WHERE
TO FIND THEM™

BOWTRUCKLE

FANTASTIC BEASTS

BEASTS
AND WHERE TO FIND THEM™

BILLYWIG

MORTLAP

FANTASTIC
BEASTS
AND WHERE
TO FIND THEM

DOXY

ERUMPENT

FANTASTIC
BEASTS
AND WHERE
TO FIND THEM™

240274

PORPENTINA
GOLDSTEIN

MACUSA

FANTASTIC BEASTS

SWOOPING EVIL

FANTASTIC BEASTS

THUNDERBIRD

FANTASTIC
BEASTS
AND WHERE
TO FIND THEM™

RUNESPOOR

FANTASTIC BEASTS
AND WHERE TO FIND THEM

GRAPHORN

FANTASTIC
BEASTS
AND WHERE
TO FIND THEM™

FANTASTIC
BEASTS
AND WHERE TO FIND THEM

DUNG BEETLE

FANTASTIC
BEASTS
AND WHERE TO FIND THEM™

MOONCALF

BABY GRAPHORNS